The Seesaw

Welcome to Animal Square!

Hi,
I'm Monkey.

Monkey is playful and curious. He always has good ideas.

Hi,
I'm Kitty.

Kitty is a little shy and cautious. She doesn't like to get her clothes dirty.

Hi,
I'm Mouse.

Mouse is very small, but she is very brave.

Hi,
I'm Giraffe.

Giraffe is thoughtful.
He thinks before
he speaks.

Hi,
I'm Rabbit.

Rabbit is always busy.
She loves to play
with everyone
at the same time.

Hi,
I'm Dog.

Dog is a dreamer.
He is very calm.

Copyright © 2022 Clavis Publishing Inc., New York

Originally published as *Samen op de wip* in Belgium and the Netherlands by Clavis Uitgeverij, 2012
English translation from the Dutch by Clavis Publishing Inc., New York

Visit us on the Web at www.clavis-publishing.com.

Animal Square, The Seesaw (softcover edition) written by Judith Koppens and illustrated by Eline van Lindenhuizen

ISBN 978-1-60537-833-6

This book was printed in September 2023 at Dream Colour Printing Ltd., No.9C,
North Puxinhu Avenue, Tangxia Town, Dongguan City, Guangdong Province, China.

First Edition
10 9 8 7 6 5 4 3 2

The Seesaw

Judith Koppens &
Eline van Lindenhuizen

Clavis

NEW YORK

"I'm going to the playground," Giraffe says.
"I'm going to have lots of fun."

At the playground, Giraffe takes a look around.
What will he do first?
"I don't really feel like swinging or sliding," he thinks.
"I know! I want to play on the seesaw!"

"Oh, but wait! I can't play on the seesaw by myself.
I can only play on the seesaw with someone else."
Just then, Mouse comes by. Maybe she'll want to play
on the seesaw with Giraffe.

"Hi, Mouse," calls Giraffe.
"Will you play on the seesaw with me?"
"Sure," says Mouse. "That sounds like fun!"
Upsy-daisy! Mouse hops onto the seesaw.

"Uh-oh!" says Mouse.
"I think you're too heavy. Look, I can't go down!"
"I'm not too heavy," Giraffe says.
"You're too light. Look, I can't go up!"

Mouse scrambles down from the seesaw.
Then she sees Monkey.
"There's Monkey," Mouse says.
"He's bigger and heavier than I am.
Why not ask Monkey to play on the seesaw with you?"

"Hi, Monkey," calls Giraffe.
"Will you play on the seesaw with me?"
"Sure," says Monkey. "That sounds like fun!"
Alley-oop! Monkey leaps onto the seesaw.

"Uh-oh!" says Monkey.
"I think you're too heavy. Look, I can't go down!
Not even when I jump!"
"I'm not too heavy," Giraffe says. "You're too light.
Look, I can't go up!"

"I have an idea!" says Monkey, standing on his seat.
"There's Dog. He's bigger and stronger than I am.
Why not ask Dog to play on the seesaw with you?"

"Hi, Dog," calls Giraffe.
"Will you play on the seesaw with me?"
"Sure!" Dog wags his tail. "That sounds like fun."
Heave-ho! Dog climbs onto the seesaw.

"Uh-oh," says Dog.
"I think you're too heavy. Look, I can't go down!"
"I'm not too heavy," Giraffe says.
"You're too light. Look, I can't go up!"

Giraffe looks very sad.
"I guess I can't play on the seesaw with anyone."
Mouse, Monkey, and Dog want to help their friend
and they devise a plan.

"Together we're not too light!" Monkey says happily.
"And Giraffe is not too heavy!" shout Dog and Mouse.
"Hooray!" cheers Giraffe.
"All together, we can do it!"

See you again soon!